This book belongs to:

. . . .

. . . .

. . . .

. . . .

Put that fat cat on a diet!

by Nancy Scott Ansley
illustrated by Heather Cooper

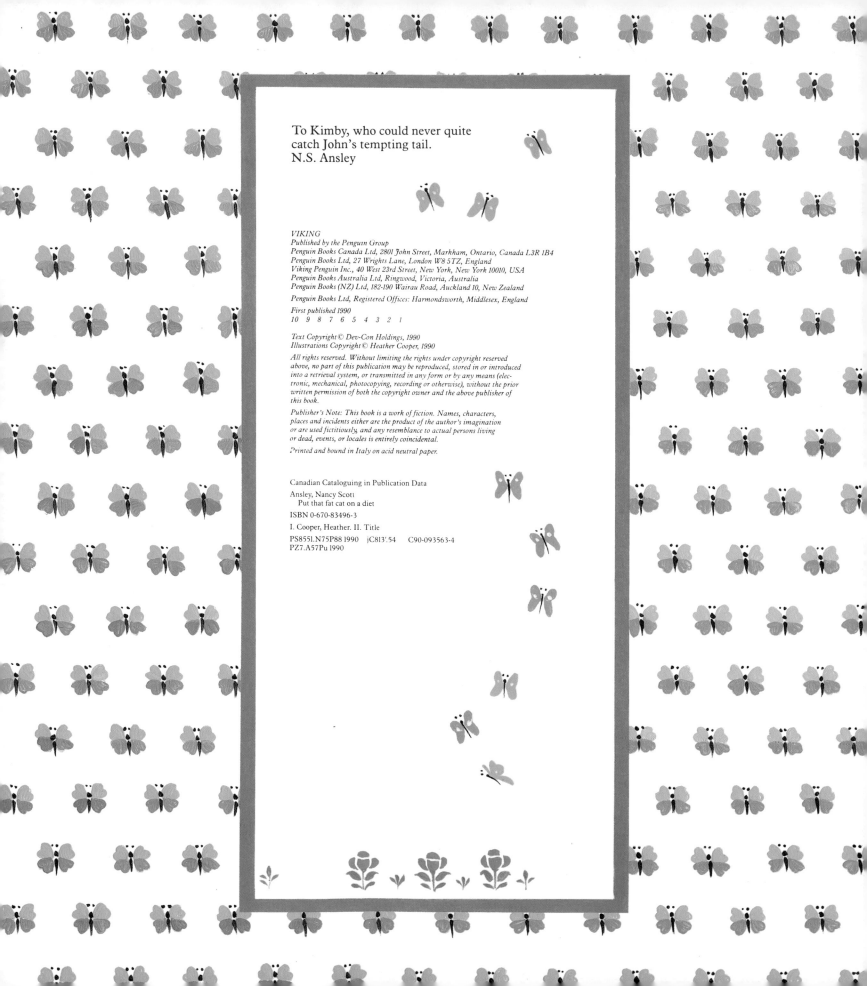

To Kimby, who could never quite
catch John's tempting tail.
N.S. Ansley

VIKING
Published by the Penguin Group
Penguin Books Canada Ltd, 2801 John Street, Markham, Ontario, Canada L3R 1B4
Penguin Books Ltd, 27 Wrights Lane, London W8 5TZ, England
Viking Penguin Inc., 40 West 23rd Street, New York, New York 10010, USA
Penguin Books Australia Ltd, Ringwood, Victoria, Australia
Penguin Books (NZ) Ltd, 182-190 Wairau Road, Auckland 10, New Zealand

Penguin Books Ltd, Registered Offices: Harmondsworth, Middlesex, England

First published 1990
10 9 8 7 6 5 4 3 2 1

Text Copyright © Dev-Con Holdings, 1990
Illustrations Copyright © Heather Cooper, 1990

Canadian Cataloguing in Publication Data

Ansley, Nancy Scott
    Put that fat cat on a diet

ISBN 0-670-83496-3

I. Cooper, Heather. II. Title

PS8551.N75P88 1990   jC813'.54   C90-093563-4
PZ7.A57Pu 1990

Once there was a fat cat called John.
John loved to eat.

He ate cat food, dog food, and even people food.
"Oh, John," said Melissa. "You're so fat! Why can't
you be thin like other cats?"
But John just purred and kept on eating.

John loved to get dirty. He stepped in puddles.
He rolled in leaves. And he sat down in mud.
"Oh, John," said Mom. "Why can't you be clean
like other cats?"
But John just purred and tracked his muddy paws
across the floor.

Most of all, John loved to sit in the garden. He watched the squirrels, the birds, and the butterflies.

"Oh, John," said Ben. "Why don't you play and hunt like other cats?"

But John just purred and stretched out in the sun.

One day Dad said, "We should put that cat on a diet!
"John, you're too fat. You're too dirty.
And you're much too lazy. Go outside
and get some exercise. It's time you
changed your ways."

But John didn't want to exercise, and he
didn't want to be thin or clean. He would
find someone who would like him just the
way he was.

And so, with his head held high,
John left home.

Soon he came to a busy park. A kindly
woman was sharing her lunch with
the squirrels.

"Have some too," she said to John.
And he did.

Then, with his stomach full and his
heart content, John settled down to
snooze in the afternoon sun.

When John woke up and looked around, it was
nearly dark and everyone was gone.

He remembered his warm bed at home and set
off to find a place to spend the night.

Feeling a little scared, he left the park.
His stomach was beginning to growl.

John walked and walked and walked
until he came to an alley. It was
long and dark, but he could smell
something delicious. He peeked
around the corner and saw two big
garbage pails. He tiptoed in.

John tried to jump up. He tried to
stretch up. But try as he might, he
could not reach the top of the pail.
So he pushed against it with all
his strength.

There was a tremendous bang,
and the alley came alive!
"Scram!" yelled a man.

And so, with an empty stomach and a heavy heart, John crept away. He was hungry, he was dirty, and he was miserable. He missed his warm bed.

At home the next morning, John's family
wondered where he could possibly be.
They were really worried. He had never
stayed out all night before! He had
never missed breakfast before! They
looked in all his favourite places,
but John was nowhere to be found.

"Oh, poor John," said Melissa. "I hope he's coming home. He's my best friend. Remember all the times we dressed up and played house? He's such a gentle cat."

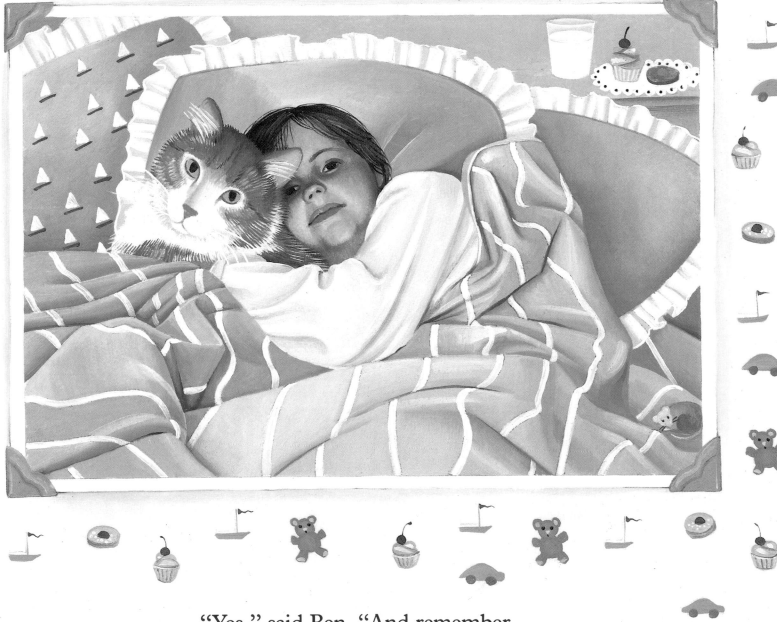

"Yes," said Ben. "And remember
how he always snuggles in bed with
me? He's such a cosy cat."

"And remember the time," said Dad, "when
John chased that huge dog out of the garden?
He certainly is a brave cat."

"Well, we've got to find him," said Mom.
And off they went down the street.

"John! John!" They called as they walked
along. But John was nowhere to be seen.
Sadly, they went home.

There on the doorstep was a wet, dirty bundle.

"John!" they cried. "You're home!"
They took him inside and dried him off, and then
they gave him the biggest, most delicious breakfast
he'd ever eaten. No one said anything about diets
or exercise.

"Well, John," said Dad. "You may be spoiled, and you may be a nuisance sometimes, but we wouldn't know what to do without you."

As for John, he just curled up and purred louder than ever.

"You know, John, maybe you *should* go on a diet."